Things My Mother Taught Me

by Katherine DiSavino

A SAMUEL FRENCH ACTING EDITION

SAMUEL FRENCH

FOUNDED 1830

SAMUELFRENCH.COM

MUSIC USE NOTE

IMPORTANT BILLING AND CREDIT REQUIREMENTS

THINGS MY MOTHER TAUGHT ME was first produced by The Rainbow Dinner Theatre in Paradise, Pennsylvania on June 5th, 2012. The play was produced by David DiSavino and Cynthia DiSavino, with direction by Scott Russel and Katherine DiSavino. Set, Decor, and Costumes were designed by Cynthia DiSavino with Technical Direction by Scott Russell, Lighting Design by Jeff Cusano and Props by Jimmy "2step" Cosentino. The production stage manager was Scott Russell. The cast was as follows:

OLIVIA	Kate B. Diem
KAREN	Cynthia DiSavino
CARTER	David DiSavino
GABE	Jonathan Erkert
LYDIA	Casey Allyn
WYATT	Joe Winters
MAX	Scott Russell

CHARACTERS

OLIVIA - late 20s

KAREN - her mother

CARTER - her father

GABE - late 20s

LYDIA - his mother

WYATT - his father

MAX (male or female) - late 50s, building Super

SETTING

An open, two bedroom apartment in Chicago, in a neighborhood in the beginning stages of gentrification.

For my parents, who taught me everything I know.
For their parents, who taught them.

ACT ONE

Scene 1

(Lights up on the mostly empty living room/kitchen area of an apartment in Chicago. It's an open space, brightly lit, in a building that has seen better days, in a neighborhood that is slowly building itself back up. But there's a fresh coat of paint on the walls, and an air of hopeful possibility about the place.

A few unopened boxes are placed against the back wall, each labeled: "GABE'S BOOKSHELF," "OLIVIA OFFICE," "KITCHEN CRAP" and so on.

Also, there's an oversized armchair stuck in the front door.

A siren sounds outside.

OLIVIA KEEGAN, *late 20's, full of energy, dressed in "moving day" denim, is currently trying to yank the chair into the apartment. This is not easy. She pulls. She pushes. She tugs. She wrenches. Nothing happens.)*

OLIVIA, This is why people hire movers, isn't it? *(to the chair)* Isn't it?

(She pulls her hair up into a pony tail. She takes an aggressive stance. She rubs her hands together. She runs towards the chair and tries to shove it into the hallway.)

Hi-ya!

(It doesn't budge.

She pushes it again, her hands on the back of the chair. Her feet slide out beneath her. She runs in place for a moment, trying to push the chair.

7

A change of tactics. She grips underneath the seat cushion and pulls. She pulls harder. One last huge heave. **OLIVIA** *loses her grip on the bottom of the chair and lands on her back.*

She lays on the floor. She throws a small fit, still on the floor.

MAX MIROWSKI, *the building super, appears in the doorway behind the chair.*)

MAX. *(to the chair, clucks)* Uh-oh.

OLIVIA. *(sits up)* I'm sorry – who are –

MAX. Max. Mirowski. Building Super. Nice to meet you.

OLIVIA. Oh! *(She stands.)* Hi! Nice to meet you too.

MAX. You got a problem here, yes?

OLIVIA. Oh, well. Yeah. The chair seems to be stuck.

MAX. Yeah. Uh-oh. *(beat)* Well. Happy Move-In!

  (He turns to leave.)

OLIVIA. Oh – uh – Max? Do you – do you think you could help me at all with –?

MAX. *(perfect English)* I'm sorry. My English is not so good. I don't understand what you're saying.

OLIVIA. I see.

MAX. Here's a good thing to remember, new tenant: if it's not a problem with building, it's not my problem.

OLIVIA. So – you don't think a chair stuck in the door is a problem with the building?

MAX. No. It's a problem with your chair. Should be smaller.

OLIVIA. Great. Thanks.

MAX. You are welcome! Oh, and, is that your truck downstairs? With the gangly man unloading the things?

OLIVIA. Oh! Yes. That's us –

MAX. Uh-oh.

OLIVIA. Uh-oh? What do you mean, uh-oh?

MAX. In this neighborhood, maybe you don't leave so many things on the sidewalk if you don't want someone to walk away with them very fast.

OLIVIA. Oh? *(realizing)* Oh! Oh dear!

MAX. As I said, Happy Move-In! Oh – and, ah – nice chair.

(**MAX** *exits.*)

OLIVIA. *(calls after him, not insincerely)* Thank you?

(**OLIVIA** *runs to the window and tries to open it. It doesn't budge. She tries playing with the locks. It still doesn't budge. She has a quiet, succinct tantrum, manages to get the window open, and sticks her head outside.*)

(calling) Gabe? Gabe? HEY! Sir! Sir – I can see you. That is not up for grabs. That's right. Up here. Keep walking! GABE?

(**GABE LAWSON**, *late 20's, appears in the door frame behind the armchair. He is carrying a large box.*

As if having a chair block the entrance to your apartment were the most normal thing in the world, he climbs over the back of the chair, steps on the seat, and hops down into his new apartment.)

GABE. You calling me?

(His voice startles her. She slams her head on the bottom of the window sash.)

OLIVIA. Holy mother of –

GABE. Whoa. That looked like it hurt –

OLIVIA. Did it? *(stares at him, then at the chair)* Did you just walk on the chair?

GABE. I climbed over it to get in–

OLIVIA. Gabe! It's brand new!

GABE. It's blocking the entire door, Liv. How else am I supposed to get in here? Pole vault?

(He puts the box down on the floor and crosses to her.)

Let me see your head.

OLIVIA. We're never going to get that chair out of the door.

GABE. *(inspecting her head)* Oh, sure we will. Eventually. Is this where it hurts?

OLIVIA. Yes.

GABE. *(kisses the spot)* Come on, grumpy. I love you!

OLIVIA. *(grumbling)* I know it.

GABE. Happy Move-In Day!

OLIVIA. Happy Move-In. I'm sorry I'm kind of –

GABE. It's okay. There's a chair stuck in the front door of our brand new apartment.

OLIVIA. No. There's a *brand new* chair, that we picked out together, and drove *eight hundred miles* across the country, stuck in the front door of our brand new apartment.

GABE. So I guess this is a bad time to remind you that my old chair, currently sitting in the truck downstairs, would have fit through the door just fine?

OLIVIA. That smelly, old, flea infested, *orange* chair is not coming into the apartment. I told you that in New York and you snuck it into the truck anyway.

GABE. Shhh. You're upset. Don't say things you don't mean.

OLIVIA. Why would we bring that chair in here when we have a perfectly wonderful, *new*, not smelly, neutral colored chair that is a thousand times better –

GABE. But stuck.

(OLIVIA *wails.*)

Come on, Liv! It's not a big deal. It's just a chair.

OLIVIA. It's not just a chair! This is *our* chair! It's our first chair that we picked out together, and we can't get it into our new home!

GABE. Olivia –

OLIVIA. And not only can we not get it into our new home, we can't get anything *else* into our new home. Oh no! What if this is a sign, Gabe?

GABE. It's a sign that we should bring my orange chair up.

OLIVIA. Gabriel. This is a big deal.

GABE. The chair?

OLIVIA. *You and me!* Our first apartment. Our first chair. I just wanted everything to go smoothly.

GABE. That chair means a lot to you, doesn't it?

OLIVIA. Our chair. Our chair, Gabe. It's such a nice chair!

Look at how nice it is.

(*She pets the chair.*)

GABE. Alright. Come on. We'll give it the ol' heave-ho one more time.

(*They move to the armchair, each grabbing the underside of it.*)

Pull on three. One.

OLIVIA. Two.

GABE. Three!

(*They pull as hard as they can. They lose their grip at the same time. They both fall backwards.*)

(*They lie on the floor together. A beat.*)

OLIVIA. Why didn't we hire movers, again?

GABE. You said it was bourgeois and we both needed the exercise anyway.

OLIVIA. I said that?

GABE. Yes, you did, pretty.

OLIVIA. That chair is going to stay there. Forever.

GABE. (*Sits up. Affecting an over-the-top air.*) Oh my goodness! This looks like a job for Carlton Prettyouse of HGTV! Now, hmm. Let me see. Oh! We could just put the couch next to the door, and make this the seating area. Do you think we can put the TV in the middle of the room? A little off center? Oh no. That would look weird, wouldn't it?

OLIVIA. No, I think that could fit the current aesthetic nicely.

(*She sits up and covers her face with her hands.*)

GABE. (*back to normal*) Uh-oh. Is someone hungry? Because you will be very happy to know that I did manage to carry up a case of the best cereal in the world.

(*He pats the box he brought in.*)

A full case of Cocoa Bites, just for us.

OLIVIA. I can't believe you brought an entire case of cereal from New York.

GABE. Well, I didn't think I would be able to find it in Chicago. Olivia, this is one of the few cereals left that still have cool toys in the boxes. Race cars, plastic decoder rings, stickers – breakfast doesn't get much better than that. Also, it turns your cereal milk into chocolate milk like magic.

OLIVIA. Well, I'm very glad the Cocoa Bites made it in safely. What else is left in the truck?

GABE. Most of our clothes. The couch. The bed. The Futon. The Mattress. Your desk, and every other piece of furniture we own…you know what? Let's just move into the truck! An urban mobile home – what do you say?

OLIVIA. Hm. Parking our house might get complicated.

(She stands.)

GABE. But think of all the new neighborhoods we'll be able to try out! So much better than being stuck in one place, right?

OLIVIA. And if any relatives come to visit – we can just drive off!

GABE. Very funny.

OLIVIA. Speaking of which – isn't it kind of weird we haven't heard from anyone today?

GABE. *(a little too off hand)* No. That's not weird. Why would that be weird?

OLIVIA. Usually your mom calls four times a day just to say "How's my baby boy?!"

(OLIVIA makes kissy noises and coos at GABE, teasing.)

You just moved half-way across the country, so I kind of counted on her checking in at least ten times by noon.

GABE. Huh. Yeah. Well. *(a beat)* Actually. Have you heard from your parents at all? About anything?

OLIVIA. No. Why?

GABE. Oh. No reason – just wondering. *(a beat)* They knew today was the move, right?

OLIVIA. I only told my dad ninety times. Maybe everyone is just trying to give us a little space.

GABE. Wouldn't that be something? I mean, we are twenty-eight – so it's kind of about time, but still –

OLIVIA. Baby – *you* are twenty-eight.

GABE. Ah, here comes the rub.

OLIVIA. *(playfully moving around the apartment away from him)* *I* am a spry twenty-seven –

GABE. *(following her)* – and a half –

OLIVIA. – wildly attractive and sought after by most –

(She coyly dodges away from his grasp.)

GABE. – taken and loved by one man only

(He catches hold of her and pulls her towards him.)

OLIVIA. Twenty-seven and a half and very much in love.

(She kisses him.)

GABE. That's my girl.

OLIVIA. Oh shoot! Did you leave the truck open downstairs?

GABE. Yeah. Why?

OLIVIA. GABE!

(OLIVIA sprints to the window and practically half hangs out of it to get a good view of the truck.)

(GABE laughs.)

GABE. Olivia. We just moved from New York. You seriously think I left the back of our truck open while we were both upstairs?

OLIVIA. Don't laugh at me! You've done dumber things –

GABE. Like what?

OLIVIA. Like saying – "Let's just push the chair a little harder, Liv, I'm sure we can make it fit."

GABE. Ha-ha.

OLIVIA. I just wanted to make sure, because I met the building super, and he casually mentioned that our neighborhood is crawling with criminals.

GABE. Sounds like every neighborhood in New York. Did the Super say anything about the chair?

OLIVIA. Yes. He said, "Uh-oh."

GABE. Uh-oh? Anything else?

OLIVIA. Yes. "If it's not a problem with the building, it's not my problem."

GABE. Did he at least offer any advice on how to get it out?

OLIVIA. No. Ugh! Gabe. The truck is still full. How are we going to get everything in here?

GABE. We can still carry some of the smaller things up from the truck!

(**GABE** *starts towards the front door and begins to climb over the chair.* **OLIVIA** *grabs his hand and hauls him off of it.*)

OLIVIA. *(panicked)* No! We can't just climb all over this thing like a – like a pack of monkeys.

GABE. A pack of what, now?

(*He moves towards the window.*)

OLIVIA. What are you doing?

GABE. Problem solving.

(*He disappears into the bedroom.*)

There's a fire escape in here! Hey! Liv!

OLIVIA. *(suddenly wary)* What?

GABE. *(reappearing in the bedroom doorway)* Since we're a pack of monkeys, why don't we climb down the fire escape and bring the rest of the smaller stuff up?

OLIVIA. What?

GABE. This way, we don't have to go anywhere near the new chair.

OLIVIA. What about the bed and everything? We can't just haul a mattress up the fire escape under one arm.

GABE. One thing at a time, my dear! C'mon!

(*He grabs her hand and starts pulling her to the bedroom.*)

OLIVIA. Whoa! Gabe! The fire escape isn't just a flight of stairs. You're only supposed to use it in an emergency.

GABE. Olivia. I thought the preservation of our brand new chair meant more to you than this. Think of all the times we would have to step on it if we do this the other way. With our *dirty, smelly, city shoes.*

OLIVIA. Gah! FINE. Let's do this, monkey!

(**OLIVIA** *marches into the bedroom.* **GABE** *follows after her, laughing. We hear a window open, and the sounds of the city outside get louder for a moment. There's some clanking offstage as* **GABE** *clumsily climbs out onto the escape. There is a beat while the apartment stands empty. Then, heavy footsteps from the stairwell are heard.*)

WYATT. *(off)* How many floors up are they? Hail Mary and Joseph!

LYDIA. *(off)* Don't stop, Wyatt! Keep climbing! If I stop moving, I'll never be able to start again!

WYATT. *(off)* Hey little lady, get your hands off my butt!

LYDIA. *(off)* I'm helping! I'm propelling you forward!

(**WYATT** *and* **LYDIA LAWSON** *appear on the landing, behind the armchair.* **WYATT** *is a good-natured man in his sixties who loves his son, marriage, golf, and beer – not always in that order.* **LYDIA** *is a retired psychologist, well dressed, and always thinking of what's best for her only child.*

LYDIA *is carrying an enormous purse filled with various cleaning supplies.*

WYATT *is carrying the largest package of multiple paper towels you have ever seen.*

They contemplate the chair in the door frame. They confirm that they have the right apartment number. They look back at the chair.)

WYATT. *(regarding the chair)* Huh. Interesting idea.

LYDIA. Oh Wyatt, for goodness sake. It's not a burglar alarm. The children have gone and wedged a piece of furniture into the door.

WYATT. Well, that's nothing a little elbow grease can't fix!

(He rolls up his sleeves and puts his shoulder to the chair, trying to push it into the apartment. As he pushes, he sinks lower, and lower behind the back of the chair.)

(From behind the chair:) It's stuck.

LYDIA. Good assessment, darling. Hold still.

(She takes off her shoes and steps onto the back of her unseen husband, using him as a stepping stool to swing her leg daintily over the back of the chair, then the other, then onto the seat and into the apartment.)

Hello!! Surprise! Gabe! How's my baby boy?!

WYATT. *(slowly stands, holding the small of his back)* How the heck they manage to get this thing stuck like this?

LYDIA. Wyatt, I don't think they're here! Gabriel? Olivia? Hello?

WYATT. I mean, they must have just jammed it in there.

(He is trying to climb over the back of the chair. It's difficult.)

LYDIA. Honestly – did they just run out and leave their apartment standing wide open in an unfamiliar city? We could have been criminals.

WYATT. Uh –

(He is stuck halfway over the back of the chair.)

LYDIA. *(sees him, begins laughing)* We wouldn't have made very good criminals, huh?

(She crosses to him and helps him into the apartment. They hug. He's left a rather large, dirty shoe print on the chair.)

Oh! Look what you did, you old man.

WYATT. Whoopsa-daisey!

LYDIA. Go wet down a dish towel. Olivia is going to have a fit if she sees this.

WYATT. What's the big deal? It's just a little dirt.

LYDIA. *(tries to brush the dirt off with her hands)* They got this chair together.

WYATT. I can't find a dishtowel.

LYDIA. Wyatt, for goodness sakes, open up some of the boxes and find one.

WYATT. It's just a chair. Olivia's a big girl. She won't have a hissy if it's got a little dirt on it.

LYDIA. Wyatt –

WYATT. *(He starts looking.)* I'm looking, I'm looking.

LYDIA. The first furniture piece a couple purchases together is momentous. A lot of time and effort goes into selecting the right thing. And your whole apartment takes shape around that item. It will always be your first "x".

(He finds a bag of potato chips and opens them, his search for the dish towel forgotten.)

WYATT. Lydia, I love you. But that sounds like a big, steaming pile of horse hoo-ha.

LYDIA. Don't be such a grump. You remember our first – ?

WYATT. *(too quickly)* Of course I do.

LYDIA. You do?

WYATT. Oh yeah. Of course. How could I forget – that thing. It's just, you know. What I'm saying is – kids these days. They don't look at their…furniture the way we did.

LYDIA. You sure loved sitting on it, didn't you.

WYATT. Sure did! Why – it was the most comfortable… thing in the world.

LYDIA. *(smacks his chest)* It was a coffee table, you unromantic old poop.

WYATT. *(playfully fending her off)* Ah, yes, the coffee table! How I loved that coffee table.

LYDIA. Oh, you.

(They kiss. A loud thud from the bedroom scares them. They freeze, afraid for a moment that perhaps another home invasion is taking place with actual burglars.)

OLIVIA. *(off, out of breath)* Hurry up. I'm already there.

GABE. *(off – grunting noises as he struggles to climb to the fire escape landing.)*

(LYDIA and WYATT, minds firmly in the gutter, look at each other horrified.)

LYDIA. *(stage whisper)* He knew we were coming today! This is just rude.

WYATT. Well, Olivia didn't know we were on the way. When we were young, you found it hard to contain yourself, too – remember?

LYDIA. Wyatt –

OLIVIA. *(off)* Let me help –

GABE. *(off – straining)* I can do it – I'm almost there –

LYDIA. Maybe we should go!

(She motions towards the door.)

WYATT. You kiddin' me? I'm not climbing Mt. Everest again.

(He crosses to the chair and sits in it.)

You said Gabe wanted a weekend full of surprises.

(The kids grunt offstage.)

(He puts his fingers in his ears.) Well, surprise!

OLIVIA. *(off)* Want me to pull it all the way in?

GABE. *(off)* Yeah – get a good hold on it, though.

(LYDIA is horrified. She motions to WYATT, unable to speak.)

GABE. *(off)* That tool bag is a lot heavier than it looks.

OLIVIA. *(off)* Good thing I carried it up almost the entire way, then, huh?

GABE. *(off)* Shut up.

OLIVIA. *(enters the living room)* You shut up.

(GABE follows OLIVIA into the living room. OLIVIA is carrying a box, GABE, a large bag of tools. OLIVIA sees LYDIA first. She drops her box.)

Oh my God!

LYDIA. Oh my God!

WYATT. *(fingers still in his ears)* You kids all done breaking the new place in?

GABE. *(simultaneously confused and horrified)* What? Wait – what?

LYDIA. Surprise!

OLIVIA. *(to GABE)* Surprise?

(WYATT *hugs* OLIVIA.)

GABE. *(to* OLIVIA, *nodding vigorously.)* Surprise! I had no – *(to his mother, winking at her)* I had NO idea you were going to drive here! *(hugs her)* Wow – Mom. *(a whisper)* You are REALLY early.

WYATT. *(crosses to GABE)* My boy!

GABE. Dad. Hey!

(*They hug.*)

LYDIA. *(hugs* OLIVIA) You look – lovely. What were you two doing? We didn't interrupt anything, did we?

OLIVIA. What? *(slow realization)* OH! Oh – no, no, no. We – because of the chair – so I – we went down the fire escape to get some –

GABE. We tried out a different route to the van.

OLIVIA. Just trying to stay on track with moving day!

LYDIA. *(to* WYATT) See? We weren't interrupting anything! I told you so!

GABE. Nope, not a thing.

(GABE *puts his arm around* OLIVIA. *They smile, trying to be comfortable. They realize they are touching. And that his parents thought they were having sex. They jump apart.*)

OLIVIA. Wow. Wow, guys. Wow. So, you drove all this way to –

LYDIA. To help, of course!

WYATT. *(about the chair)* Looks like we should have gotten here a little earlier, though – huh, son?

GABE. Oh yeah. You sure should have.

OLIVIA. *(notices the dirt on the chair)* The chair! OH MAN! The chair!

LYDIA. *(to* WYATT*)* I told you.

OLIVIA. Oh no. Oh no. Gabe –

> *(She points at the dirt.)*

GABE. Dad. Did you –

> *(*WYATT *takes his shoe off and wipes it on his shirt.)*

WYATT. What?

GABE. The – the shoe print? Olivia's just a little sensitive about dirt getting on the new chair.

OLIVIA. *Our* new chair, Gabe. Lydia – did you see that?!

LYDIA. I told him you would be upset.

GABE. Liv, it'll come out. We'll just wipe it off! No big deal.

OLIVIA. I'm sorry. I'm sorry, I'm so – agh. And I'm sorry you had to climb over the stupid thing, Wyatt.

WYATT. Almost didn't make it, to tell the truth!

OLIVIA. Lydia – do you think it'll come out?

> *(*OLIVIA *and* LYDIA *inspect the foot print.* OLIVIA *is very clearly having a minor panic attack and trying valiantly to conceal it.)*

GABE. You guys, really, it's not –

WYATT. He's right, you know. What's a little dirt compared to the fact that it's stuck in the doorway?

GABE. Dad. Now is not the best time –

OLIVIA. *(in total despair)* We'll never get it unstuck!

LYDIA. This never would have happened if you had hired professionals to help you move in. I told you two to hire movers. Olivia, didn't I mention that would be a good idea?

OLIVIA. *(Unpacking boxes in the kitchen. Through clenched teeth:)* You sure did, Lydia.

LYDIA. So where are they?

GABE. We wanted to save money and do it ourselves, Mom.

LYDIA. And look what happened. That's all I'm saying.

GABE. Mom, don't.

LYDIA. Gabriel, you're bringing two separate lives together in a brand new city! This is a very big deal. You should be taking it seriously.

(**OLIVIA** *slams a cabinet door.*)

GABE. We are, Mom. We are taking it very, very seriously.

WYATT. Of course you are, Gabe! Of course he is, Lydia. We just – we figured you would need an extra set of hands. Especially since you got twice the amount of crap to move.

(*He wanders to the door and inspects the armchair.*)

LYDIA. And when have we ever *not* helped you move into a new apartment?

GABE. (*a bit pained*) You've been there every single time, Mom.

LYDIA. Darn right we have! From college until now! Why would I tarnish my perfect record?

(**OLIVIA** *slams a cabinet door.*)

WYATT. She wouldn't dream of it!

(*He moves to the tool kit and takes it back with him to the door. Throughout the next section he fiddles with the door frame and the chair quietly, trying out different tools as he attempts to pry the chair from the frame. No one notices.*)

LYDIA. That's right! My baby boy just moved to Chicago with his lady!

OLIVIA. His lady needs cleaning supplies. Gabriel? Come help me find cleaning supplies.

LYDIA. Open your eyes, Olivia, they are right in front of you! I brought them. I can scrub down the cabinets while you unpack!

OLIVIA. No, Lydia – please. It's okay. You just drove here from Connecticut. Relax. Do you want some water?

LYDIA. I'm fine! The drive was a piece of cake.

WYATT. That's cause I did all the drivin'!

OLIVIA. You guys must have gotten up mighty early.

LYDIA. *(no big deal)* Two a.m.

OLIVIA. And you didn't stop at all?

LYDIA. Straight through.

GABE. Straight through? Seriously? I thought I told you to – *(He catches himself.)* That's a little crazy, Ma.

LYDIA. It's how you young kids do it, isn't it?

OLIVIA. Listen, Lydia, you and Wyatt should go and take a nap at your hotel.

(A beat.)

LYDIA. Hotel?

(A beat.)

GABE. You – you did book a hotel, didn't you?

LYDIA. Why would we book a hotel? You've got two bedrooms right here!

GABE. Mom. *(under his breath)* This is not what we discussed.

LYDIA. Hotels in Chicago are extremely over-priced. It's like they think this is New York City or something. Ridiculous.

GABE. Mom.

OLIVIA. Gabe?

WYATT. And don't even get us started on how much we spent on gas.

GABE. Mom – you and Dad – that is to say, Olivia and I, we –

LYDIA. Oh, sweetie, it'll be fun! A big slumber party. And think of the manual labor you'll get out of us. *(with a sly smile)* This is a very big weekend, after all.

GABE. *(stiffly)* Yes. It is.

OLIVIA. Gabe?

GABE. Mom – I –

LYDIA. *(gives GABE a hug)* I'm so excited! Oh! We'll even put together the extra bed ourselves. You don't have to worry about a thing.

(A beat. The sound of sawing. Everyone looks at **WYATT**, *who has found a handsaw and is using it on the door.)*

GABE. Dad – no!

OLIVIA. THE CHAIR!

(She moves towards the chair and **GABE** *swiftly grabs her and pulls her into a straight jacket sort of hug without taking his eyes off of his father.)*

WYATT. *(sawing the door frame as he talks)* You know, Gabe, if there's one thing I've learned in sixty five years, it's that there's always a way to make something work.

(He has sawed off an enormous portion of the door frame. He tosses it to the ground with the saw and reaches under the chair to give it a tug. The chair pulls easily into the room.)

There we go!

*(***MAX**, *the super, appears in the doorway. He looks at the sawed-away portion of the door frame, then at the chair, then at* **OLIVIA**.*)*

MAX. Uh-oh.

*(***MAX** *shakes his head.)*

(There is a collective beat of silence.)

WYATT. So! Which bedroom is ours? This old man needs a nap.

(blackout)

Scene 2

(Several hours later. At rise, it looks like a few more items in the truck have been brought in – though the apartment is still suspiciously empty.

LYDIA *is in the kitchen, cleaning. She is currently standing on a chair and Windex-ing the top of the refrigerator.* **WYATT** *has a dry mop in one hand and a beer in the other.)*

LYDIA. It's so dusty up here.

(LYDIA scrubs harder. **WYATT**, *with dry mop in hand, wanders over to a wall sconce that is not working. He fiddles with it.)*

It's really disgusting.

(She scrubs again. A beat. She sighs. A beat. She scrubs more viciously.)

I mean, I can't believe the landlord let them move in with the apartment in this condition. This is black mold. It has to be.

(GABE enters with an end table.)

WYATT. Not yet! She's not finished!

GABE. Are you serious?

LYDIA. No furniture until we're done cleaning, Gabriel. Why don't you go get groceries? And take that back down to the truck!

(GABE sighs, grabs the end table and exits.)

WYATT. When are you going to let us bring up the rest of their furniture, Lydia? The truck is still full down there.

LYDIA. We have to make sure the whole apartment is properly cleaned first. Olivia never would have thought to clean up here. It takes a lot of living in apartments before you remember to clean the top of the fridge. That's what my mother taught me. When you move into a new place, always clean the top of your refrigerator. And always, *always* buy a new toilet seat. You don't know what could be on one, and you know *exactly* what's been on the other.

WYATT. You know what my mother always said? Out of sight, out of mind.

LYDIA. Your mother was a lunatic. Hand me another paper towel.

WYATT. In a second.

LYDIA. The sooner you dry mop, the sooner we can wet mop, and the sooner we can unload the truck.

WYATT. You sure you don't want to take a power hose to the floor after we wet mop?

LYDIA. Don't be cute.

WYATT. Lydia, cool your jets.

LYDIA. I just – I really need another paper towel, Wyatt. Please.

WYATT. Okay, okay.

(*He crosses to the counter and grabs the roll of paper towels, then hands it to her.*)

You doing alright? Do you need to lie down?

LYDIA. No – they'll be back soon with the groceries, and I'll have to get dinner started.

WYATT. I thought Olivia said she was going to cook tonight.

LYDIA. Mmm. Yes.

WYATT. Now, Lydia –

LYDIA. She isn't used to cooking for so many people. She'll need a hand.

WYATT. Lydia –

LYDIA. I'm here to help!

(*A beat. She begins to scrub again.*)

She needs my help.

WYATT. Get down from there.

LYDIA. I'm not done –

WYATT. Get down from there right now.

LYDIA. Alright, fine.

(*She climbs down.*)

What?

WYATT. Olivia can cook dinner. Gabe can help, and you can relax.

LYDIA. They need help.

WYATT. Lydia, they're twenty-eight. They're grown adults.

LYDIA. I'm worried, okay? Are you happy? I'm worried about them, and I – I don't know. I thought I was okay with this.

WYATT. You're having second thoughts about what they're doing?

LYDIA. Am I old fashioned?

WYATT. You are *old*.

LYDIA. Wyatt –

WYATT. (*softening*) Come here.

(*He holds her.*)

LYDIA. Is this how all the kids are doing it now? Moving in before they're married…or even engaged?

WYATT. They love each other, Lydia.

LYDIA. Of course they do – any idiot can see that, Wyatt.

WYATT. Then what's the problem? If they love each other, and they're happy, why shouldn't they take this next step?

LYDIA. Because this *isn't* the next step! That's the whole thing. An engagement ring is the next step. A wedding is the one after that – and *then* you get an apartment together. That's how we did it – and that's how our parents did it –

WYATT. He's not going too far out of order, Lydia.

LYDIA. I know that he's planning on proposing this weekend. I know – it's just – what if everything goes wrong? What if she says no?

WYATT. I imagine that he would be very hurt.

LYDIA. And then what? Does she move out? Does he? Right now, the biggest commitment they have made is the one to their apartment.

WYATT. Lydia – how long have Gabe and Olivia been seeing each other now?

LYDIA. What? I don't know – since college, I suppose.

WYATT. Junior year of college, Lydia. They've been together for seven years. We dated for six months and then got engaged. Got married the next year.

LYDIA. And?

WYATT. They keep choosing to be with each other. I'm just saying, after a year and a half, I was stuck with you!

LYDIA. Wyatt!

WYATT. Married or not, they're making the same decisions we made. But they're doing it their way – not ours.

LYDIA. *(sniffles)* You're a nice, romantic old man.

WYATT. They're going to be okay, my love.

LYDIA. You know, every now and then, I remember why I'm glad I married you.

WYATT. Good. Now, get me another beer.

LYDIA. And then I forget all over again.

WYATT. And some duct tape.

LYDIA. A beer I can do. You're on your own for the tape.

(**WYATT** *crosses to the door and opens it, just as* **OLIVIA** *and* **GABE** *arrive on the landing, out of breath and laden down with groceries.*

OLIVIA *really, really needs to pee.)*

WYATT. Here come the pack mules!

OLIVIA. *(crosses to the kitchen counter)* Oh wow! You're still cleaning? I thought you were just going to do a quick floor-sweep while we got the groceries –

LYDIA. Oh, no. You've got to clean much more thoroughly than that before you bring any of the furniture in.

OLIVIA. We need to clean the top of the fridge before we bring the furniture in?

LYDIA. Certainly.

OLIVIA. Okay. Well, it's just – it's getting kind of late in the day, and we've got a lot to still bring up from the truck–

GABE. Yeah. Like – basically everything we own.

LYDIA. Don't you two worry! We're almost done! We just need to finish scrubbing the kitchen. *(a beat)* Then we'll dry mop the living room – and then wet mop it – and then dust, sweep, mop, and mop both bedrooms. Again. Then we can bring in the furniture.

OLIVIA. *(overwhelmed)* Oh. Is that all? Well. We'll get started in a second. If you guys would excuse me –

(She starts towards the bathroom.)

LYDIA. *(frantic)* Where are you going?

OLIVIA. …the bathroom?

LYDIA. No! No! The other very good piece of advice is that you should always, ALWAYS replace the toilet seat when you move into a new apartment.

OLIVIA. Okay. Well – I kind of really need to take care of this now –

LYDIA. Absolutely not. On a scale of one to ten, how bad is it right now?

OLIVIA. I'd say I'm a solid nine and a half.

(She edges towards the bathroom door.)

GABE. Mom. Let Olivia pee.

WYATT. *(sotto)* Son, you don't want to get in the middle of this. Beer?

LYDIA. *(counters* **OLIVIA,** *incredulous) Nine and a half?* And you can't wait for me to run to the hardware store to pick you up a new one?

OLIVIA. A new toilet!?

LYDIA. A new seat! Focus!

OLIVIA. Lydia – *please.* This is serious.

LYDIA. NO! Think of all of those foreign germs – my mother would roll over in her grave.

OLIVIA. Okay, well, I'm about to pee on the floor, so think of all of *those* foreign germs.

GABE. MOM! What about a Pee-Pee Pad?

OLIVIA. A what? No. What?

GABE. A Pee-Pee Pad. It's sort of like those seat protectors–

WYATT. Except eight inches thicker –

GABE. We took this road trip once, and I really had to take a –

OLIVIA. Okay. Stop. Yup. Got it.

LYDIA. Gabriel, that is a GREAT idea. Okay! Here's the plan! Olivia, we will make a pee-pee pad!

OLIVIA. We?

WYATT. It's a very involved process.

LYDIA. Requires two people minimum. But it'll be a nice, thick, barrier for you to *hover* over whilst you take care of business.

OLIVIA. Lydia – this sounds a little –

LYDIA. DO YOU WANT TO USE THE RESTROOM OR DON'T YOU?

OLIVIA. Okay! Okay – let's do this!

LYDIA. Wyatt! Paper me.

WYATT. *(throws the roll of paper towels to her)* Go get 'em tiger.

(**LYDIA** *pulls* **OLIVIA** *into the bathroom.*)

GABE. *(yelling)* I'm so sorry! I love you!

WYATT. That's not gonna help you one bit.

GABE. I know. Can I have that beer, now?

WYATT. Yup.

(**GABE** *and* **WYATT** *drink their beers in silence. A moment.)*

GABE. Is she just going to stay in there with Olivia?

LYDIA. *(offstage)* I'm not looking!

GABE. Dad –

WYATT. And there's something I can do?

GABE. We're gonna need a lot more beer.

(WYATT *glances at the bathroom door and tiptoes over to* GABE.)

WYATT. *(sotto)* Does she – you know – suspect anything yet?

GABE. Between the chair being wedged in the door and Mom's toilet seat phobia, I think we've done a pretty good job of keeping her distracted.

WYATT. You got the ring on you?

GABE. *(a beat – very proud of himself)* I hid it in the van! No way she'll find it – even if she snoops.

(*They clink beers and drink.*)

Hey – Dad? Thank you for coming.

WYATT. You think we would miss our son proposing to the girl of his dreams? *(Brooklyn accent)* Fugget about it.

GABE. *(laughing)* It means a lot to me that you're here. Hopefully Olivia will feel the same way when her –

WYATT. She doesn't know you invited her parents?

GABE. *(happy)* No. I didn't tell her. *(panic)* Is that bad?

WYATT. Gabe – don't you think you should have at least prepped her?

GABE. But it's a surprise. Her mom doesn't even know I'm proposing. I just talked to her dad, asked permission, invited them up but said to keep it a secret –

WYATT. Wait. Karen doesn't know?

GABE. *(happy)* Nope. *(panic)* Is that bad?

(*The toilet flushes. Sound of water running in the sink.* LYDIA *reenters the living room.*)

LYDIA. There. All better.

OLIVIA. *(enters. At a loss.)* I – I …

LYDIA. You're welcome, dear! Now, Wyatt, we need to go get a new seat for them so we don't have to go through this again.

OLIVIA. Yes. Please. Let's not do this again.

WYATT. But I didn't finish fixing the door yet.

LYDIA. You can do that when we get back. Olivia, will you be okay starting dinner without me? Maybe you should wait –

OLIVIA. I think I'll be okay.

GABE. Do you want me to give you money for the –

WYATT. Oh, no, son. We'll spring for this one.

LYDIA. Oh! It'll be our first housewarming present to you!

WYATT. You can thank us later. C'mon Mrs. Pee-Pee Pad. Gabe. Keys?

(**GABE** *tosses* **WYATT** *a set of keys.* **WYATT** *and* **LYDIA** *exit.*

A beat.)

GABE. You look *so* beautiful right now.

(*He goes to hug her. She puts her hand on his forehead, arm extended.*)

OLIVIA. Don't even try that Casanova bull on me. I just peed in front of your mother. The last thing I want right now is a cuddle from the child that came out of her uterus.

GABE. Fair enough. Beer?

OLIVIA. Absolutely.

GABE. *(hands her a beer)* You know she means well.

OLIVIA. I do. I just wish she would mean well a little less forcefully.

GABE. If she didn't like you, she would have just let that nice little butt of yours hit the seat.

OLIVIA. I can't imagine a better way to show your affection for your son's girlfriend than some good old fashioned bonding time.

GABE. Hey –

OLIVIA. No need to get defensive, here. Lord knows my mother has a few quirks of her own, too.

(**OLIVIA** *clears a large space on the kitchen counter and begins unpacking the groceries.*)

GABE. *(snorts)* Yeah. A few.

OLIVIA. What's that supposed to mean?

GABE. Come on, Liv. Remember last spring when we went to visit your parents and we got there early?

OLIVIA. *(cautiously)* Vaguely.

GABE. And your mother was in a panic when we got in and had to run out to Kinkos –

OLIVIA. We were ahead of schedule –

GABE. She had to go to Kinkos to pick up the PRINTED PAMPHLET she made for our visit.

OLIVIA. It wasn't a pamphlet, it –

GABE. Olivia. It was a pamphlet. Tri-fold. On glossy paper – it detailed every single family event we would be attending for the entire weekend. Every minute, mapped out to a tee.

OLIVIA. *(straightening some groceries)* There were blocks for free time, too! My mother is just very organized, okay? There's nothing wrong with that!

GABE. *(stops her from anxiously straightening more groceries)* I'm sorry, Liv. You're right. There's nothing wrong with that.

OLIVIA. I'm glad I'm nothing like her. *(sheepishly)* I organized the groceries.

GABE. I see that. Can we put them away, now?

OLIVIA. Yes.

GABE. *(hugs her)* I love you. And I'm really sorry my parents assumed it would be okay if they stayed here with us for their visit. I should have mentioned something when – *(He catches himself.)*

OLIVIA. When what?

GABE. *(clears throat, begins putting groceries away)* When I was talking to my dad earlier…today. But I can't just kick them out. They would be so hurt. Besides, it's not that big of a deal, right? It's not like we're all sleeping in the same room.

OLIVIA. No, you're right.

GABE. There. Silver lining, see?

OLIVIA. The real silver lining is that my parents didn't decide to show up this weekend, too.

(OLIVIA *pulls out a knife from one of the boxes.*)

(GABE *freezes.*)

(*She begins preparing dinner.*)

GABE. Yeah. Ha. That would be weird, huh? Uhm, by the way – how did your mom take the news?

OLIVIA. The news?

GABE. – about us moving in together?

OLIVIA. Right. Well –

GABE. Olivia. No.

OLIVIA. Well, I kind of told her. I told her the way we always tell each other things.

GABE. Passive agressively?

OLIVIA. More like just "passively", but yeah.

GABE. What did you say, exactly?

OLIVIA. Well, she was all, "So – big move to Chicago, huh?" And I said, "Yeah. It's exciting!" And then she said something about hoping my apartment was okay, and I told her it's big enough for two people to live in –

GABE. (*covering his face*) You can't be serious –

OLIVIA. And then she said she hoped I wouldn't be lonely and I told her I wouldn't be, because I have you! See? So, she totally knows. Also, I told my dad flat out. So he probably clarified everything.

GABE. Olivia, what the hell?

OLIVIA. Gabe –

GABE. When we talked about whether or not we should move in together, the thing we kept coming back to was that we're both mature adults –

OLIVIA. We are! We totally are –

GABE. Adults who love each other and want to share more of our lives with each other, right?

OLIVIA. Absolutely – but –

GABE. And now here we are! Moved in. And you're keeping this a secret from your mother?

OLIVIA. It's not a secret. I did tell her. It's just – you know, I didn't detail it for her or anything. It's how we communicate!

GABE. You gotta be kidding me. Are you a freaking teenager?

OLIVIA. Gabe–

GABE. Am I going to find you sneaking out the bedroom window tonight to meet up with your friends in the Regal Cinema parking lot?

OLIVIA. Listen – I'll call her and tell her everything. I promise.

GABE. Why not tell her now? Would she not be okay with us living together?

OLIVIA. No. It's not that. It's just – sometimes, she doesn't react to things the way you'd think.

GABE. What do you mean?

OLIVIA. It's hard to explain –

GABE. Try.

OLIVIA. She just doesn't want me rushing into anything – serious.

GABE. But – she's okay with us living together?

OLIVIA. Oh, sure. As long as she doesn't think we're too – serious. That's why I thought it might be easier if my dad broke the news to her first.

GABE. "Broke the –" Olivia – this is *happy* news. This isn't something you *break* to someone. We *are* serious about each other. That's something you shout from the rooftops!

(*He climbs on top of the kitchen counter.*)

OLIVIA. Gabe what are you – get down!

GABE. I JUST MOVED IN WITH OLIVIA KEEGAN! I CAN'T WAIT TO SEE WHAT KIND OF WEIRD BATHROOM HABITS SHE HAS.

OLIVIA. Gabe – oh my God. The walls are thin!

GABE. *(shouting over her)* SHE HAS A BEAUTIFUL SMILE, NICE HAIR, A FEW MOMMY ISSUES AND A VERY PATIENT BOYFRIEND. I LOVE HER, AND I DON'T CARE WHO KNOWS IT! OH – AND HER BUTT IS REALLY AWESOME!

(WYATT *opens the front door, holding a large toilet seat in its box and stands there with* LYDIA, KAREN KEEGAN *[mid-late 50's, impeccably dressed] and* CARTER KEEGAN *[late 50's, always seems to be holding an iPhone in one hand].*

They are all looking at GABE, *standing on the kitchen counter.*

GABE. *(a beat)* Hello. *(He clears his throat. He climbs down from the counter.)*

KAREN. Olivia!

OLIVIA. Mom?

CARTER. Hiya, kiddo!

OLIVIA. What are you guys doing here?

GABE. Olivia, is that any way to treat guests in our new home?

KAREN. Are you two going for a minimalist look in here?

OLIVIA. All the furniture is down in the van, Mom. We were just finishing up cleaning.

(OLIVIA *and* KAREN *hug.*)

KAREN. Well. I very much like *your* new home.

GABE. Wow. What a surprise that you guys drove all the way up here this weekend.

(He winks at CARTER.)

CARTER. *(nudges* GABE) We just thought we should – you know – eh – *(nudges again)* Drive up and visit our little girl – eh, eh? *(Nudge. Nudge.)*

KAREN. Carter, is there something the matter?

CARTER. EH? Nope! *(waves his iPhone at* **WYATT***)* Hey – Wyatt this is the application I wanted to show you. It's a level! On the phone!

WYATT. Get out of town.

CARTER. I will not, sir! Come on, look at this!

(CARTER and WYATT retreat to study the iLevel.)

KAREN. Well.

LYDIA. *(nervously)* Well!

OLIVIA. Well.

GABE. Well! Mom! How about we put that new toilet seat on?

LYDIA. That's a great idea! Be right back, Karen.

KAREN. *(sincerely)* A new toilet seat. That's the first thing you should buy whenever you move into a new place.

LYDIA. That's what I said too!

GABE. Mom. C'mon.

(He picks up the toilet seat and pulls his mother into the bathroom.)

*(*KAREN *smiles. It is a tiny bit forced. She is making an effort to be cool with everything. She is not.)*

KAREN. So! Wow! This is the big move, huh? I'm ready! *(She holds up a tape measure and several Ikea catalogues.)* When you said your apartment was big enough for two people, you weren't kidding!

OLIVIA. Mom – is everything okay?

KAREN. Okay? Of course.

OLIVIA. You seem a little upset, is all.

KAREN. Why on earth would – Olivia. Stop that. I'm fine. What have I always told you? When you were growing up – what did I always say?

OLIVIA. Stop dressing like you're going to a picnic?

KAREN. Not that.

OLIVIA. Always use protection when you're having sex?

WYATT. *(looking up from the iPhone)* Uh. I should see how they're doing with that toilet. Gabe and tools. I mean screws. I mean – they probably need my help.

(He retreats to the bathroom, leaving **CARTER** *holding the iPhone and looking a bit nervous.)*

KAREN. I always said wait until you're at least thirty to get married. I think a young woman needs time to experiment.

CARTER. *(looking up from the phone)* Can I go help with the toilet seat, too?

KAREN. No. Because we are a family. And families have discussions as a group.

OLIVIA. Experiment?

KAREN. Yes – try things out! Live with your boyfriend. See if he's the right one. Live with all of your boyfriends. If it doesn't work out, don't be hurt – just try something else.

OLIVIA. Try something else? Like, find another boyfriend and live with him for a while? Or just sleep around a lot while I'm living with Gabe?

CARTER. Uh. Yeah. This is girl time. So. I'm gonna –

(The bathroom door opens. **WYATT**, **LYDIA** *and* **GABE** *appear and all gesture for* **CARTER** *to make a run for it.)*

*(***CARTER*** *walks very quickly to the door and disappears inside.)*

*(***KAREN*** *and* **OLIVIA** *don't notice.)*

KAREN. Please stop twisting what I'm trying to say.

OLIVIA. I just want to make sure I understand, Mom.

KAREN. I'm not trying to get into an argument with you. I'm simply trying to say that I wholeheartedly support your decision to experiment with your current living situation.

OLIVIA. There's that word again! Why do you keep throwing that around? This isn't some kind of science test, Mom. This is – serious.

KAREN. Well, it can't be *that* serious, can it? Since you didn't even tell me about it.

OLIVIA. I did! On the phone. Kind of.

KAREN. You certainly implied that you two might be co-habitating, but I assumed you didn't want to say anything more because you were feeling it all out. To see if it's right for you. Which I support! See what's most comfortable.

OLIVIA. Most comfortable? I'm not trying on shoes, Mom.

KAREN. You are incredibly young.

OLIVIA. I'm twenty-seven –

KAREN. Exactly. I've been in your position. I was in a committed relationship way before I should have been –

OLIVIA. You got married before you even finished college –

KAREN. I said yes to the first guy in college who asked me, because that's what *my* mother told me to do. And it didn't work out, did it? It ended in divorce. But I learned from that heartbreak, and I became more comfortable in my own skin, and then I met your father, and we got married and we had you. And I've always tried to be open with you about my mistakes. So you wouldn't repeat them.

OLIVIA. Can we not talk about this right now?

KAREN. I don't understand why you didn't tell me the whole truth. "I'm making a career move to Chicago with my man friend!" I've told you I don't mind that kind of thing. I'm very open-minded! I used to own a motorcycle – a moped – and I love listening to pop music!

OLIVIA. Mom –

KAREN. I bought you your first brassiere! You used to tell me about all the guys you dated. I can barely get eight words out of you about Gabe –

OLIVIA. Maybe it's because every time I try talking about him you change the subject to whatever stupid new renovation you're doing to the house! Did you ever think about that?

KAREN. Olivia.

OLIVIA. No. You do. Especially when we were first dating and I was dying to tell you all about him –

KAREN. You were in college, Olivia. He was your first real boyfriend. He's been your only real boyfriend. I was worried, okay? I didn't want you to take him too seriously – So *I* never did.

OLIVIA. That's the truth! And you made it very clear to me you didn't care to hear very much about it. So, yeah. I didn't directly tell you we were moving in together. I didn't know how you'd react and obviously I was right in thinking you might have an issue with it. Now, if you'll excuse me. I'm going to make dinner.

(There is a long beat of silence. Both women are stewing.

The bathroom door opens. **GABE, LYDIA, WYATT** *and* **CARTER** *peer out.*

WYATT *clears his throat.)*

WYATT. Seat's on! What's for dinner?

OLIVIA. I was just going to do a little soup and salad.

*(**CARTER** goes to the windows. He opens one. He looks out.)*

CARTER. *(yelling out the window, friendly)* It's a Juke! A Nissan Juke – new model. Very zippy. *(to* **KAREN***)* There's a man out there admiring our car, Kare-bear!

OLIVIA. Oh, God. *(runs to the window)* HEY! HEY YOU! YEAH – That car has a security alarm and my mother is a lawyer! KEEP WALKING!

KAREN. How much research did you actually do about this neighborhood before you moved here?

GABE. Uhm – well. We looked at some Google street view images. And there are a bunch of really hip coffee places around here with great reviews. It's – you know – it's an up-and-coming neighborhood …

KAREN. *(snapping)* Did you look at crime statistics? *(takes a deep breath)* Are you sure that this is the best place to –

OLIVIA. Please stop.

KAREN. I'm just trying to have a *conversation* with Gabriel, Olivia. Because we *do* talk, you know. Don't we, Gabe?

GABE. *(very confused)* Yeah. Of course we –

KAREN. SEE?

WYATT. How about we cook some meat for dinner?

OLIVIA. I don't have any of the pans unpacked yet –

LYDIA. Most of the kitchen stuff is still out in the van with everything else.

KAREN. Doing a thorough clean before moving everything in?

LYDIA. Of course.

KAREN. *(slightly comforted)* Good. Who knows what was in this place before.

OLIVIA. I'll cook up a big slab of bacon in the morning for you, Wyatt. How's that sound?

WYATT. Sounds pretty darn good.

KAREN. In the morning?

WYATT. Yup! Lydia and I are staying with the kids.

(He slaps GABE's back.)

GABE. *(trying to alleviate some of the tension in the room)* Yay!

CARTER. Huh. That's funny! We're planning to stay the night here, too.

OLIVIA. What?   **GABE.** I'm sorry?

KAREN. What on earth are you talking about? In the car you said you'd already had a hotel lined up.

CARTER. Yeah! Here.

KAREN. CARTER.

OLIVIA. Daddy. No.

CARTER. What? They have two bedrooms - there's plenty of room for us all here. Why would we spend money on a hotel?

LYDIA. That's what I said!

OLIVIA. Dad - it's just –

KAREN. This is turning into quite a little weekend, isn't it?

OLIVIA. Mom –

KAREN. Oh, no. It's fine, Olivia. *(sniffs)* We'll find a hotel somewhere and head out after dinner. You can stay here together.

GABE. No way, Karen. You and Carter should absolutely stay here with us tonight.

KAREN. How nice!

OLIVIA. Yeah. Gabe. I don't really think that's the best –

GABE. Really. You guys can take the futon, my mom and dad will have our bed, and Olivia and I will sleep on the air mattress.

KAREN. That's sweet, but we don't want to impose, Gabriel.

LYDIA. Oh, stay, Karen! You won't be imposing on the kids at all! And, you know, it'll give us all a chance to talk and catch up.

KAREN. Well, it certainly does seem like I have a lot of catching up to do, doesn't it?

LYDIA. What – what do you mean?

OLIVIA. *(tight-lipped)* Mom. Would you please help me make dinner?

(**OLIVIA** *begins chopping salad.* **GABE** *gets out salad bowls.* **WYATT** *gets pan out and empties cans of soup into it.*)

KAREN. *(puts her arm around* **GABE**'s *neck – a half hug half choke-hold)* Well, it seems that Olivia here doesn't think I've made a very good effort to get to know your son over these past few years.

OLIVIA. This is hardly the time or the place to be discussing this, Mom.

(**KAREN** *lets* **GABE** *go and sits down, pouting.*)

(**CARTER** *and* **WYATT** *look at each other. They really don't like arguments and both can sense one coming on.*)

WYATT. Carter and I are gonna go get the kitchen table out of the van.

CARTER. Yup. And the chairs. Be back soon!

> *(They grab the truck keys off the counter and practically run towards the door.)*

> *(**KAREN** picks up a big knife on the counter and starts ferociously [and loudly] chopping celery [or whatever vegetable they are having with dinner].)*

> *(The noise makes the men move faster.)*

CARTER *(cont.)* *(to **GABE**)* Every man for himself, kid.

> *(He shuts the door behind him as he and **WYATT** exit.)*

KAREN. *(gesticulating with the knife)* I don't know if you know this, Lydia, but I was married once before. When I was *very* young. And neither one of us knew what we really wanted, and the entire thing was a total disaster. We were not ready to get married, and we certainly were not ready to live together.

OLIVIA. Mom. What the hell –

KAREN. Olivia, you've been dating the same boy since you were twenty-one. You are *young*. You both are. There may be other things you both want to experience. You don't need to take this move-in so seriously. If this option doesn't work out – no big deal. *You aren't married!*

LYDIA. But they soon will be!

> *(Outside, there is a screeching of tires and shouts from the sidewalk below.)*

GABE. MOM.

LYDIA. *(covers mouth)* Oh.

OLIVIA. Gabe? What?

KAREN. *(to **LYDIA**)* What did you say?

LYDIA. *(crying)* He's proposing this weekend.

KAREN. *(crying)* You are too young to get married!

> *(Shouts from the hallway. Footsteps pounding up the stairs.)*

(OLIVIA *and* GABE *stare wordlessly at each other.*)

WYATT. *(off)* THE TRUCK!

LYDIA. What on earth –

(LYDIA *moves to the door.* WYATT *appears, panting.* CARTER *is behind him, also panting, on the phone. They enter the apartment.*)

WYATT. *(panting)* The truck – the truck is –

CARTER. *(on the phone)* We want to report a car theft –

KAREN. Oh my God – what happened?

CARTER. *(on the phone)* Yes, it's a U-Haul van – *(to* OLIVIA*)* Do you have the paperwork – they need the plate information.

OLIVIA. WHAT?

LYDIA. For the love of Pete, Wyatt, SPIT IT OUT!

WYATT. Someone stole the moving van!

OLIVIA. What? Mom? What?

(She begins to cry.)

KAREN. Oh God. Liv – it's okay, sweetie –

(She hugs her daughter.)

Quick, find the paperwork for your dad – is it in your purse?

(LYDIA, KAREN *and* OLIVIA *frantically search for the truck lease.*)

GABE. No.

WYATT. When we got downstairs –

GABE. NO. No, this can't be happening.

WYATT. There was nothing we could –

GABE. *(freaking out)* Dad. Everything was in there.

(He points to OLIVIA, *then to his hand, indicating the engagement ring.)*

EVERYTHING. EVERYTHING. EVERYTHING WAS IN THE VAN BECAUSE I HID EVERYTHING IN THE VAN.

WYATT. Gabe –

GABE. Mom just ruined my proposal, and now this?

WYATT. She did what, now?

LYDIA. *(crying)* IT WAS AN ACCIDENT.

KAREN. Here it is!

> *(She hands the paperwork to* **CARTER***, who begins reading it off into the phone.)*

GABE. NO. I'm finding that Van! I HAVE TO FIND THAT VAN!

OLIVIA. Gabe, where are you going?

GABE. I'M FINDING THE VAN!

> *(***GABE*** runs out.)*

> *(***WYATT*** and ***CARTER*** look at each other and nod.)*

WYATT. We're going with Gabe to find the van, too.

LYDIA. Are you crazy?

WYATT. They can't have gotten far. It's a big van. Carter has a zippy car. We're doing it. C'mon, Carter.

CARTER. *(to* **KAREN** *and* **OLIVIA***)* Love you – *(to the phone)* No, not you, the plate number is U84, 7RT –

> *(***WYATT*** and ***CARTER*** exit, ***CARTER*** still giving information to the police. They leave the door open.)*

> *(***LYDIA***,* ***KAREN*** *and* ***OLIVIA*** *stand there, motionless.)*

> *(There is a beat.)*

> *(***MAX*** appears in the doorway.)*

MAX. Hey – where's your truck?

> *(***OLIVIA*** wails and cries louder.)*

Uh-oh.

> *(Blackout.)*

END ACT ONE

ACT TWO

(One hour later. **KAREN** *sits on a blanket on the floor, empty salad bowls in front of them. The soup pot sits in the middle of the blanket. Two empty bottles of wine lay on the blanket as well.* **KAREN** *is drinking from her glass.* **LYDIA** *is asleep in the chair.* **OLIVIA** *paces by the windows, checking her phone every few minutes.)*

OLIVIA. It's been over an hour. Where are they? And why won't Gabe answer his phone?

KAREN. Would you put your phone down and come here? You hardly touched dinner, and you're beginning to wear a track in the floorboards.

OLIVIA. Aren't you the least bit worried that none of them have contacted us?

KAREN. Olivia, they aren't going to call to say they've come up empty handed.

OLIVIA. How do you know they're empty handed?

KAREN. Because they haven't called.

OLIVIA. Gabe always calls me. Or texts. Always. Not that you'd know that.

KAREN. I refuse to have an argument right now. You are worried and distraught and are channeling all of your emotions through your anger at me.

OLIVIA. What are you, a lawyer or a psychiatrist?

KAREN. Trust me. They'll let us know as soon as they find something. Right now, the three of them are probably driving all over Chicago's South Side looking for moving vans.

OLIVIA. I feel like I'm going to be sick.

KAREN. Olivia –

OLIVIA. Mom. I don't want to be reasoned to or cooed at right now. Everything Gabe and I own just drove off.

KAREN. Thank goodness you moved the chair in before it happened. Where else would we nap?

OLIVIA. It's new.

KAREN. It's a very nice chair, Olivia. Very tasteful.

OLIVIA. Gabe and I picked it out. Together.

KAREN. You did? Oh, Olivia. That's so nice!

OLIVIA. What is wrong with you? An hour ago you were trying to convince me to engage in partner-swapping and now you're practically leading a round of Kumbaya. To be quite honest, it's freaking me out.

KAREN. Liv –

OLIVIA. Could you maybe lecture me about my choice of neighborhood again?

(MAX *enters the front door carrying a bottle of Krupnik –* *a Polish honey vodka. He also has shot glasses.*)

KAREN. Max. You're back!

MAX. I found the honey vodka I was telling you about. I also brought the shot glasses, because I thought maybe yours were stolen, Olivia.

OLIVIA. They were.

MAX. It is the least I can do! You fed me dinner. Also, I feel bad because all of your things were taken. This never happens here.

OLIVIA. This afternoon you told me that people would take things if we left them out on the street.

MAX. *(perfect English)* I'm sorry? I don't understand. My English is not too good. *(beat)* Ladies? Shots?

KAREN. She certainly needs one.

OLIVIA. You know what, Mom? I'm actually feeling a little upset right now, and I don't think alcohol is going to fix that.

MAX. That is silly. Alcohol cleans all kinds of wounds. Even emotional ones. *(He pours shots.)* I see you two are still grouchy with each other.

KAREN. Not me. I'm fine. I'm being extremely supportive, actually, but apparently it's freaking my daughter out.

OLIVIA. Only because it's uncharacteristic and creepy.

MAX. Ok. Good! Karen, you have a shot, too.

KAREN. No, Max. I don't want one.

MAX. I'm sorry? I don't understand. My English –

KAREN. Fine, fine. Shots.

MAX. Shots!

> (MAX *pours four shots.*)
>
> (*He hands them to the women.*)
>
> Za milosc, mlodosc i dobra awanture.*
>
> (*They all drink.*)

LYDIA. (*asleep*) Mmm!

MAX. Ok. Now you talk.

OLIVIA. There's nothing to talk about.

KAREN. Actually, there's quite a bit to talk about, but we don't want to drag you into this, Max.

MAX. (*pouring himself another shot*) It's okay. My English is not too good, so you can talk.

OLIVIA. This is literally the worst night of my life.

KAREN. Would you please stop being so damn dramatic.

OLIVIA. I am NOT being dramatic.

MAX. You are being a little dramatic. So your truck was stolen – hey! No big deal.

OLIVIA. Well, my boyfriend and my father are both missing, too.

MAX. No big deal! They are all fine. They will call when they have something to tell you.

KAREN. Just what I said. Thank you, Max.

MAX. (*pouring another shot for* OLIVIA *and* KAREN) Yes, okay. Drink this. Chlusniem bo usniem!**

---

* Pronouciation: "Zah mee-loast lodos ze dobra ah-van-tura." Meaning: "To love, youth and good arguments."

** Pronouciation: "hlooshnyem boooshnyem." Meaning: "We drink, if we not gonna sleep."

(They all take another shot.)

KAREN. Olivia, I'm honestly just trying to help right now.

OLIVIA. I don't want to talk.

(Max's phone rings.)

MAX. Uh–oh! Sorry. You talk while I talk. *(He answers the phone in Polish:)* Dzien dobry?*

(MAX *steps into the hall.)*

KAREN. I know you're feeling a lot of different things, but–

OLIVIA. I'm actually just feeling angry, so clearly you don't know me that well, either.

KAREN. *(slams her shot glass on the counter)* Olivia. Enough.

(LYDIA *wakes up and sees they are in an argument. She listens to them, but periodically pretends to be asleep throughout the rest of the argument.)*

OLIVIA. Stop it! Just stop trying to be calm and collected. I know you're just as anxious as I am. And I know you're still pissed about our conversation earlier, so let's just not pretend. Everything Gabe and I have ever owned was just stolen. My computer. My clothes. My books. The dishes I picked out and the brand new mattress we just bought…

KAREN. *(quietly)* You were really excited about this move, weren't you?

OLIVIA. *(in tears)* We picked out curtains for the bedroom, Mom! He stood with me at a store for two hours. Patiently. And he helped me pick the colors. I don't even like curtains. I don't know why I wanted curtains. But we bought them. Together. And you know what the worst part is? I really, really liked them.

KAREN. I love curtains.

OLIVIA. I know you do! And I wanted to call you after we picked them out, but I didn't. Because I was worried about what you would think.

KAREN. No. Olivia, no – I think – I think curtains are a good investment.

---

* Pronouciation: "Dzh-ehn do-bri." Meaning: "Hello?"

OLIVIA. You do?

KAREN. I really do. Especially if you both picked them out together.

(A beat.)

(OLIVIA hugs her mother tightly.)

OLIVIA. Mom – I didn't know he was planning on proposing.

KAREN. You did look a bit surprised.

OLIVIA. I really love him, Mom.

KAREN. Olivia. Shh. You don't need to explain –

OLIVIA. But I do. I – I was always afraid to talk about him, because I thought you would figure it out. I've always wanted to marry him, and I've always been afraid because I wasn't sure how you'd react.

KAREN. I am your mother, and I will always think you're rushing into something.

OLIVIA. What?

KAREN. Of course I know you love him. I've suspected how much he means to you for quite some time, actually.

LYDIA. It's kind of hard to miss.

KAREN. *(wiping her eyes)* Ah, you're awake.

LYDIA. Sorry. I didn't mean to interrupt –

KAREN. No, it's good you're up. I think I'm just realizing something here, and I'm glad I have another mother for support. Olivia, I have spent your entire life trying to show you how to grow up and be a good person. You made it. You're smarter than me, and more confident than I ever was, and you have made wonderful, strong intelligent choices. Excluding the summer you were seven and wore the pocket-knife as a necklace.

OLIVIA. It was pink!

KAREN. I was so worried about you making my mistakes that I didn't see you've actually been following my advice all along.

OLIVIA. Mom?

KAREN. I told you to find yourself a man who is loving and patient and who helps out with household chores which – *(to LYDIA)* I'm assuming he does?

LYDIA/OLIVIA. He does.

KAREN. You found him. I told you to live with someone before you got married. To be sure it was right. You're doing it. And what amazes me the most is how you love Gabe. With your entire heart. That kind of love lasts a life time. You found happiness on your first try – without any advice from me. And you are so happy. What more could any mother hope for?

LYDIA. You're right.

OLIVIA. Mom? Don't you know?

KAREN. What's that?

OLIVIA. I learned that from you. To love with my whole heart. You're fierce, and loyal, and aggravating –

KAREN. Hey!

OLIVIA. And you provoke and prod and motivate and yell – but you also love. Fiercely and unconditionally. And I'm so sorry I was afraid to open up to you about Gabe – I'm so sorry I didn't –

KAREN. *(hugging her)* Shh. No, I'm the one who's sorry. I love you. And I love Gabe.

LYDIA. *(joining in on the hug)* And I love you!

KAREN. *(laughing)* And I love you, Lydia.

OLIVIA. I love you both. And *I* love Gabe, even though he isn't returning my phone calls.

(They all laugh.)

(MAX enters.)

MAX. I missed the happy part? Oh, darn!

LYDIA. My son is going to propose and she is going to say yes!

(They all cheer and motion MAX over for a hug.)

KAREN. Oh, Max. What is in that honey vodka of yours?

MAX. Honey. And distilled grains.

LYDIA. He brought the vodka? I want some.

MAX. Shots!

(He pours shots for everyone.)

(He is about to toast.)

OLIVIA. "Polish Toast!"

(They cheers and drink.)

MAX. Also, that was my brother on the phone. He is on the Chicago police force.

OLIVIA. He is?

MAX. Yes. I told him about what happened, and he and a few of his work friends are out looking for the truck.

OLIVIA. Max. Thank you –

MAX. The last thing I want is you thinking you moved to a bad neighborhood. It's not so bad here. *(to the Moms)* I promise. She will be safe here. And the boy, too. They will take care of each other, I will take care of the building, and the building will take care of us all!

LYDIA. That is surprisingly poetic, Max. I just hope you're right.

MAX. Me too. But I've seen my fair share of couples. They come and go. These two? *(He gestures to OLIVIA.)* They will be okay. With parents like you, how could they not be?

KAREN. *(touched)* Thank you, Max.

MAX. One more surprise! I will fix your door.

KAREN. Oh? You weren't going to?

MAX. I only fix problems with the building. That hole, that is a problem with your door. But, because I like you – I will fix it!

(OLIVIA starts to cry.)

Uh-oh. Did I say wrong thing? Do you want to keep the hole?

OLIVIA. *(through tears)* Even though this is a horrible day, everything is so perfect.

MAX. This is why I'm glad I had boys.

(GABE *enters the apartment.*)

Ah! This is the boy!

(GABE *walks past his mother,* MAX, KAREN, OLIVIA. *He does not look at any of them.*)

OLIVIA. Gabe?

(*They all watch him cross to the bathroom door.*)

(*He goes into the bathroom and shuts the door.*)

LYDIA. (*jumping to her feet*) GABE! Do not climb into that bathtub!

KAREN. He went in the bathtub?

OLIVIA. When Gabe gets upset, sometimes he'll lay in the bathtub.

KAREN. And take a bath?

LYDIA. No water. He just lays in the bathtub.

MAX. This is a very strange boy.

LYDIA. (*to* MAX, *gently*) It's a comfort thing. Confined spaces make him feel safe. (*pounding on the bathroom door, very angry*) Gabriel, you come out here right now and tell us what's going on.

GABE. (*off*) Mom, just leave me alone, okay?

LYDIA. No, not okay. Get out here, Gabriel.

(GABE *wrenches the door open. He stands in the doorway, arms folded. He looks a bit like a small child.*)

GABE. I'm only coming out because that bathtub is very, very small. And I couldn't remember if we had cleaned it yet or not.

LYDIA. Oh, now I can't remember, either.

MAX. You should very much clean it. (*a beat*) I will go get the tools to fix the door.

KAREN. (*gently shooing* MAX *out*) Thank you, Max. For the company and the booze.

MAX. Yes. The honey vodka I'll leave with you. (*He studies* GABE.) I think you may need it, still.

(**MAX** *exits.*)

OLIVIA. Gabe?

(**MAX** *re-enters.*)

MAX. *(a la Schwarzenegger)* I'll be back. *(He giggles.)* It's funny. Because I'm Polish, not Austrian. Nevermind.

(He exits again.)

OLIVIA. *(to* **GABE**) Are you okay? I called you, like, ten times.

GABE. I was at the police station, trying to find out if anyone was looking for the van.

LYDIA. Wait a minute. Where is your father?

GABE. What do you mean?

LYDIA. What do you mean, "What do you mean"? I mean, where is your father?

GABE. I don't know. He wasn't with me.

LYDIA. What?

KAREN. Carter and Wyatt left to go with you –

GABE. Well, they never caught up with me.

LYDIA. Karen, neither one of them has called – Wait! I don't even know where my phone is.

KAREN. They're lost in Chicago! Oh! Hold on, I'll get mine.

(The mothers, in a tizzy [and just a wee bit tipsy] begin searching for their phones. This is a very involved process.)

OLIVIA. I was really worried about you.

GABE. I'm sorry, Liv. I didn't mean to worry you. I *really* needed to find that van.

OLIVIA. We still might –

GABE. I know – it's just. I doubt our things will be with it.

OLIVIA. I just don't understand why you ran off like that.

GABE. I really don't want to have this conversation now. I'm exhausted. I just want to curl up in the bathtub and go to bed.

OLIVIA. Gabe –

GABE. Olivia, not now.

OLIVIA. And you're not even going to say anything about planning on proposing to me this weekend?

GABE. Honestly, I don't think I can anymore.

(The Moms look up from their phone search.)

(OLIVIA stares at GABE, horrified.)

(WYATT and CARTER burst in through the front door. They have their arms around each other and are singing Katy Perry's "Last Friday Night" [or some other pop song]. They don't know the words. They make some up.)*

(Oh, also, they're a little drunk. Everything they say they find really, really funny. 'Cause, you know. They're drunk.)

KAREN. What the hell?

WYATT. Oh! Hullo, Karen!

CARTER. Wyatt, everyone is back! Look!

WYATT. We are one big happy family again!

LYDIA. Where have you two been?

WYATT. Well. *(He thinks for a moment. He sits down on the chair.)* Oh, this is so comfortable.

CARTER. We tried to catch up to Gabe when he left, but we didn't! So we drove around. And we looked for the truck!

WYATT. But we couldn't find it!

CARTER. So we came back here. And that's when we saw this bar – right outside!

WYATT. *(to GABE and OLIVIA)* You have a bar right outside, you guys! This is a great neighborhood!

CARTER. And we thought: "Gee, I wonder if anyone saw anything when the truck was stolen."

WYATT. So we went inside.

KAREN. Well – did you find out anything?

CARTER. *(busts out laughing)* Nope!

---

*See Music Use Note on page 3.

WYATT. *(laughing)* No one saw anything. But when the bartender heard what happened, he gave us pickleback shots!

LYDIA. What the hell is a pickleback shot?

CARTER. Well. We thought it would be pickle juice.

KAREN. And is it?

CARTER. It is! Ya drink it after ya drink a shot of – *(giggle)* Whiskey.

WYATT. *(smacks his lips together)* Mmm. Think I need some water.

LYDIA. I'll get it. You damn fool.

(**LYDIA** *gets a glass of water for both* **WYATT** *and* **CARTER**.)

I still don't understand why you decided to just let Gabe go off on his own.

CARTER. Well, he was *so* upset about the engagement ring being in the truck. *(to* **GABE***)* You were *so* upset.

WYATT. He needed time to be alone and to think, Lydia.

GABE. Well, I have thought. And I decided to call the engagement off. For now.

WYATT. What?

OLIVIA. The ring…was in the truck?

GABE. Yeah. The ring was in the truck, okay? And so was all of our other shit. Thousands of dollars worth of our stuff. And after my conversation at the police station, I sincerely doubt we will ever see any of it again.

OLIVIA. So we'll buy new stuff –

GABE. I CAN'T.

OLIVIA. What do you mean?

GABE. I mean, between the move and buying the engagement ring, I'm broke, Olivia.

OLIVIA. Broke?

GABE. I have just about three hundred dollars left in my bank account.

OLIVIA. Wait. Hold on. That's impossible. *(beat)* Gabriel, how much did you spend on the ring?

GABE. You know what – that is none of your damn business.

OLIVIA. *(forceful)* How much did you spend on the engagement ring?

GABE. I'm not –

LYDIA. *(anxious – blurts it out)* HOW MUCH, GABE?

GABE. THREE MONTHS SALARY.

OLIVIA. *How much is that?!*

GABE *(blurting)* It's over twenty thousand –

(*A collective beat.*)

OLIVIA. ARE YOU OUT OF YOUR MIND? Why would you spend that much on a piece of jewelry?

GABE. I saw it in a magazine! That's how much you're *supposed* to spend –

OLIVIA. I DON'T EVEN WEAR RINGS.

GABE. Well, now you don't have to worry about it, do you?

OLIVIA. JESUS, GABE! I can't believe you didn't even – *consult* me on this. We could have put that money towards *anything* else – towards the wedding, towards a house –

GABE. Oh, I'm sorry that I wanted to buy you something beautiful and that I kept it a surprise from you. My bad.

OLIVIA. Gabe, that's not –

GABE. You know, and that's another thing I've lost – besides all of my money and everything I've ever owned. Ever. I've lost my one moment.

WYATT. Son –

GABE. Every guy *only* gets to do two things that are important to a wedding. They get to buy a ring. And they get to propose. That's it. Everything after that is all about the girl, looking fucking adorable, picking out floral themes and bridesmaid dresses –

LYDIA. I'm so sorry, Gabe –

GABE. And then there's the cake thing. And no matter what, the girl gets it all over her face, and still manages to look like a really hot chick in a happy commercial. Meanwhile, the groom looks like a drunken idiot. With cake on his face.

WYATT. *(impressed)* He's thought about this a lot.

GABE. My one moment to shine. My proposal. It's gone. And so's the ring. Everything is messed up, and I'm broke on top of it all. So yeah. I'm calling the engagement off. *(to OLIVIA)* I love you. But I'm not going to ask you to marry me when I don't even have enough money to cover the deductible we'll have to pay on the van.

OLIVIA. Gabe.

WYATT. Lydia. Karen. Could you please escort Olivia into the bedroom?

CARTER. Wyatt and I need a moment with Gabe. Man to Man. To Man. *(He can't help giggling.)*

(OLIVIA is near tears. KAREN puts her arm around her and walks with her into the bedroom.)

(LYDIA grabs the bottle of honey vodka and three shot glasses. She exits into the bedroom and shuts the door behind her.)

(The dads are still drunk. But drunk people can be wise. They just happen to be wise and drunk.)

WYATT. Son, sit down.

GABE. Dad, I just want to be alone for a minute, okay?

WYATT. Nope. Not okay. Sit.

(GABE sits on the arm chair.)

WYATT. *(cont.)* I'm gonna tell you something my mother said to me when I told her I wanted to propose to Lydia.

GABE. Dad, not now –

WYATT. Shut up and listen. *(beat)* First, she said, "Are you sure you wanna marry *her?*" And I said, "Yeah, Ma. I'm sure." And then she said, "You think you could love her even if you two didn't have any money?" And I said, "Of course, Ma." And she said, "Good, cause I'm not paying for the wedding."

(CARTER *wanders off. He finds instant coffee and plastic cups in the cabinet. He drunkenly begins to prepare coffee for the three of them.*)

GABE. Nan did not say that.

WYATT. Oh yes she did. So I told her I'd work two jobs to pay for the wedding myself and I had to work those two jobs for a good long while until she finally told me she was teaching me a lesson, and then she and Lydia's parents ended up paying for the whole damn thing.

GABE. I'm not sure I follow.

WYATT. Gabe, we know you want to marry Olivia. And what you said back there was one of the most responsible, reasonable things that has ever come out of your mouth. There's just one problem –

CARTER. Indeed there is.

(*He fills a measuring cup with water.*)

WYATT. You're forgetting about romance.

GABE. I love you both. Very much but –

WYATT. – I love you too, son! –

GABE. But I can't really afford to be romantic right now.

WYATT. Gabe, did you honestly ever think you were gonna have to pay for that wedding?

GABE. Dad, it's not about the damn wedding. It's about starting a new life with Olivia in debt. I don't want that. And I know her, and I know she doesn't want that either.

CARTER. (*puts the measuring cup in the microwave and starts it*) Gabe, Gabe, Gabe. There's something you gotta learn, and I know this is hard to believe – but sometimes, it's not about the women.

(*He approaches* GABE.)

WYATT. He speaks the truth.

CARTER. You should always love and respect them, don't misunderstand me, young man. But, the thing is, sometimes they're just too practical for their own good. I'll bet you right now, the women are explaining to Olivia just how *logical* you're being, and how this is ultimately a *good thing* – and you know what I say to that?

GABE. What?

CARTER. FOOEY.

GABE. Sir?

CARTER. I defy your logic! And you know what else I defy?

(**WYATT** *has wandered into the kitchen. He notices the microwave going. He opens it and discovers the [barely] lukewarm water. He then discovers the cups of instant coffee. He is delighted. He pours the water into the cups and returns the rest of the water in the measuring cup to the microwave.*)

GABE. What?

CARTER. All that bull about your one moment being taken away.

WYATT. Listen to the man, son. He may smell like whiskey and pickles, but he speaks the truth.

CARTER. You honestly think that because Lydia spilled the beans, your proposal is down the tubes? You honestly think that Olivia hasn't been speculating about when you'd propose for a while now?

WYATT. (*bringing the coffee cups over*) Cause let's be real, son. That girl is smart. And she's stuck with you for a helluva a long time. She knew this moment would come.

GABE. But she didn't know I would do it this weekend.

WYATT. But she knew you were going to do it, kiddo.

CARTER. Your moment isn't gone, Gabe.

(*The men mull this over. They all take a sip of the coffee. The drunk dads don't seem to realize it tastes AWFUL.* **GABE** *spits his back into his cup.*)

In fact, your moment just got way better.

WYATT. Oh. Oh he's got a good point.

GABE. *(trying to get the taste off his tongue)* What do you mean?

CARTER. Who wants to hear a boring proposal story? About getting down on one knee in the middle of Times Square on New Year's Eve at midnight, with a gently snow swirling around?

GABE. That sounds really n –

CARTER. *(The sound of a game show buzzer.)* EHHHH. NO ONE.

> *(He takes* **GABE**'s *coffee cup back to the kitchen.)*

WYATT. You know what people really want to hear when they swap proposal stories?

CARTER. *(answering)* Things that went horribly wrong.

> *(***GABE** *takes a seat in the chair.)*

> *(***CARTER** *sits on the arm next to him.)*

WYATT. *(pulls a carton of ice cream from the freezer and grabs three spoons)* And let's face it, son. Your mom ruined the surprise and your engagement ring was jacked in a moving van filled with your worldly possessions.

CARTER. It doesn't get much better than that.

> *(Throughout this scene, the men should eat the ice cream. It's meant to look a bit like "girl time".)*

WYATT. *(handing the ice cream to* **GABE***)* You and Olivia will be telling that story to your kids for years.

CARTER. And you know what? All of your sons will learn something from this.

WYATT. They will.

CARTER. They will learn to *always* keep your engagement ring on you at all times.

GABE. How many kids do you think we're gonna have?

CARTER. Five.   **WYATT.** Eight.

CARTER/WYATT. All boys.

> *(***WYATT** *wanders back to the fridge. He finds a can of whipped cream.)*

CARTER. When I proposed to Karen, we were in the kitchen, cooking dinner. She was sitting on the counter, looking so pretty, drinking a glass of red wine. And so I got down on one knee, and I took out the ring, and I proposed.

GABE. Carter, that's so sweet.

(WYATT *shoots whipped cream into his mouth.*)

CARTER. It was. And do you know what she did?

GABE. Said yes?

CARTER. No. She started laughing. She thought I was kidding.

(GABE, *still watching* CARTER, *opens his mouth.* WYATT *shoots whipped cream into his mouth for him.*)

And then she picked up the engagement ring – she thought it was fake, you see – so she picked it up out of the box and when she realized it was real – she dropped it down the sink!

(CARTER *laughs hysterically and tilts his head back.* WYATT *squirts whipped cream into his open mouth.* CARTER *is pleasantly surprised.*)

GABE. You're kidding me.

CARTER. Nope. I had to fish it out of the garbage disposal, but I cut my finger wide open. Blood everywhere! She had to take me to the emergency room.

GABE. Holy –

CARTER. Stitches. Eight of 'em. Still have the scar. See?

(*He holds out his finger.*)

(WYATT *puts whipped cream on it.*)

(CARTER *shrugs and licks it off.*)

WYATT. (*returning the whipped cream to the fridge*) Carter. That is one helluva war story.

CARTER. It is. (*to* GABE) And that is just one of the many reasons why you should still propose.

WYATT. Also, an engagement isn't a wedding, Gabriel. Propose to her. Save up until you're comfortable again. Then set a date for the wedding.

CARTER. Listen, it boils down to this. Do you want to marry my daughter?

GABE. Of course I do.

CARTER. Do you love her?

GABE. Yes.

CARTER. Will you eventually have more than three hundred dollars in your bank account?

GABE. Yes, of course I–

CARTER. *(takes the ice cream from* **GABE***)* Well, alright then. What are you waiting for?

WYATT. You've got a good head on your shoulders, but you gotta listen to that heart, son. Don't let anything stop you from proposing, if that's what your heart wants you to do.

CARTER. We're done with the lecture. I promise. I just want to leave you with the wise words of Beyonce Knowles. "If you like it, then you shoulda put a ring on it."

*(***WYATT/CARTER*** *sing and dance to the chorus of Beyonce's "Single Ladies".)**

GABE. *(breaking the revelrie)* But I don't have a ring!

*(***CARTER*** *puts the ice cream away.)*

WYATT. Son. Think outside the box, why don't you?

GABE. The – box. The box! That's it!

(He runs into the kitchen and pulls the box filled with the Cocoa Bites boxes in it.)

(He rips it open and begins pulling the individual boxes of cereal out, ripping them open, and dumping the cereal out onto the floor.)

WYATT. What are you –

GABE. There are prizes in here! Help me look!

---

*Please see Music Use Note on Page 3.

(**CARTER** and **WYATT** *realize what he's doing, and they begin ripping open boxes and dumping the contents out on the floor as well, searching for the plastic baggies in the cereal that contain prizes.*)

(**WYATT** *is eating cereal.*)

GABE. Don't eat the cereal Dad, find the prizes!

CARTER. Oh! What's this?

GABE. Stickers. But those are cool. Keep those. And Dad – keep looking!

(*The men rummage more.*)

(**OLIVIA**, **KAREN** and **LYDIA** *open the bedroom door. The stand watching them for a moment.*)

LYDIA. What the hell is going on?

GABE. I FOUND ONE!

OLIVIA. Gabe? Are you okay?

GABE. I'm great, Olivia. Listen – I'm so sorry about what I said earlier.

OLIVIA. Gabe, don't. It's okay. We talked and we all think that you're being really responsible. I'm not upset, I –

(**GABE** *crosses the room and grabs* **OLIVIA**. *He pulls her into a romantic, long kiss.*)

GABE. Shut up.

(*He gets down on one knee and holds up the small bag with a plastic ring inside of it.*)

(*The bag is covered in Cocoa Bites powder. He rips it open and removes the ring.*)

GABE. *(cont.)* Olivia Keegan, I have loved you since the first time you told me to stop talking to you during Chaucer class Sophomore year. I love how bright and happy your eyes are when you talk to people, I love the way you reach out to hold my hand when we're walking, I love your voice, and your hair and your smile. I love how you belch, and then laugh because you are surprised at how disgusting it sounds –

KAREN. *(embarrassed)* Oh, God, Olivia.

CARTER. That's my girl!

GABE. I love your family. And I love how you love my family. I love you. And I don't want to wait to make you mine.

OLIVIA. Gabe, I am yours.

GABE. Good. Then let's make it official. *(He clears his throat:)* Olivia Keegan. Will you please put this hilarious plastic ring on and tell me you'll marry me?

(**GABE** *holds out the plastic ring.*)

OLIVIA. It's the most beautiful plastic ring I have ever seen, Gabe. Yes. Yes, I'll marry you.

(They kiss.)

WYATT. Well, I don't know how you all feel, but I think we should celebrate the engagement by springing for some hotel rooms.

CARTER. Oh! We could check the Priceline app and see if any last minute deals opened up for tonight!

WYATT. Perfect.

(**WYATT** *and* **CARTER** *huddle to research hotels.*)

(**GABE** *and* **LYDIA** *hug.*)

(**OLIVIA** *approaches her mom.*)

OLIVIA. I love you, Mom.

KAREN. *(puts her arm around her daughter)* I love you, Olivia. *(She kisses her head.)* Just – promise me that you won't keep anything *this important* from me again.

OLIVIA. I promise. *(a beat)* Mom. I want you to be the first one to know. *(A beat. She puts her hand on her stomach.)* Gabe and I –

(**GABE, LYDIA** *and* **KAREN** *are all shocked/horrified/ worried/panicked. Is she going to say "pregnant"?)*

Are engaged.

(Everyone breathes a sigh of relief. Especially **GABE.** *)*

KAREN. OLIVIA! Whooo. You're funny. You got your sense of humor from me, too.

CARTER. *(still looking at the phone)* No she didn't.

LYDIA. We're very happy for both of you.

OLIVIA. It's nice to know that something good can come out of a day like this, isn't it?

GABE. It is.

CARTER. Found one! Ninety-nine dollars a room for tonight only! How many rooms should we get?

GABE. *(with a look to* **OLIVIA***)* I think Olivia and I are going to brave the apartment tonight without furniture.

OLIVIA. *(smiling)* Yeah.

KAREN. Just two rooms then, Carter. One for you and me, and one for Lydia and Wyatt. And Carter – make sure the rooms have king-sized beds. Who knows? You boys might get lucky tonight!

(She pinches his bum. He grins.)

*(***LYDIA** *and* **WYATT** *smooch.)*

(There is a knock on the front door.)

MAX. *(off)* Hello!

OLIVIA. Max?

(She runs to the door and opens it.)

*(***MAX** *stands in the doorway, with an armful of supplies to fix the hole.)*

MAX. I have many surprises for you.

(A truck honks outside.)

(Everyone freezes and the slowly turns towards the windows.)

GABE. No.

MAX. Yes!

(Everyone, except for **MAX***, who begins to rest his supplies by the door, sprints to the window.)*

OLIVIA. Our moving van is parked downstairs?! How is that even possible?

GABE. *(waving)* And who is that police officer waving to us?

MAX. That is my brother. He found the van and brought it here to you.

GABE. I – I don't even know what to say.

MAX. Mm. Well. Perhaps you should not say too much. The truck was empty.

GABE. What?

MAX. But you should be very happy. Because the thieves did not *burn* the truck.

WYATT. So they have the truck, but no belongings?

MAX. This is not entirely true. They have the truck. And one belonging.

(He disappears into the hallway.)

(A beat.)

(He pushes a disgusting, old, orange chair in through the door.)

Oh, look. This chair fits just right.

OLIVIA. *(laughing)* Gabe. Even criminals think your chair is horrible.

LYDIA. Gabriel. This chair is older than you are. Why the hell do you still have it?

(GABE stands motionless. He is staring at the chair. There are tears in his eyes.)

(He drops down to his knees.)

GABE. Thank you.

OLIVIA. Gabe?

(GABE crawls on his knees over to MAX and hugs him around his middle.)

GABE. Thank you.

MAX. Uh. No problem?

WYATT. What on earth has gotten into you?

GABE. *(in hysterics)* What's gotten into – ? LET ME TELL YOU! Olivia has always hated this chair. She would NEVER sit on it when she came to my apartment to visit. She didn't want me to bring it to Chicago. She won't go near the damn thing. Which is why –

(He approaches the chair. He rips off the seat cushion. He sits down on the floor, unzips the cover, and begins digging around in the stuffing.)

It made the perfect place to hide THIS.

(He pulls out a small black jewelry case. He is almost in tears he is so happy.)

(There is a collective gasp.)

OLIVIA. Oh my–

*(**GABE** opens the box. The ring sparkles inside. It's huge.)*

GABE. *(to **OLIVIA**)* You are trading in that plastic ring. Hand it over and put this on your beautiful hand.

(He jumps up and hugs her. He picks her up and spins her around. They are both ecstatic and laughing.)

(Everyone is stunned, thrilled, confused, happy.)

*(**GABE** goes to take the plastic ring off of **OLIVIA**'s finger.)*

OLIVIA. No! What are you doing?

GABE. I'm trying to give you your real engagement ring.

OLIVIA. Gabe. We are taking that ring to a jeweler first thing tomorrow morning and selling it.

GABE. *(crestfallen)* What? Why?

OLIVIA. Why? Because you're broke! Because I love my *real* engagement ring. *(She wriggles her plastic ring at him.)* Because I don't need fancy jewelry, and because you can put half of the money into your savings – where it belongs, and we'll take the other half to Ikea, and furnish our new apartment.

GABE. But – but I want you to have this.

WYATT. Son. Stop listening to your heart now and let your head do the math.

LYDIA. For the love of God let your head do the math.

GABE. *(to OLIVIA)* Are you sure?

OLIVIA. I'm positive, Gabe. You picked out a beautiful ring, love, but I'd rather you buy us a nice big bed with that money instead.

GABE. *(smiling)* A nice big bed does sound really, really nice.

OLIVIA. Yes it does.

(OLIVIA *and* GABE *kiss.*)

MAX. Okay. I fix the door tomorrow. I need to see what the Missus is up to.

(He exits, and shuts the door behind him.

LYDIA *and* KAREN *are so happy! They watch their children, mooney-eyed.*

WYATT *and* CARTER *gather their wives' belongings [and their wives] and lead them out the door [leaving the door open].*

OLIVIA *and* GABE *see their parents have left. They laugh and kiss again.*

LYDIA *and* KAREN *appear in the doorway, giggling.* KAREN *takes a picture of the couple with her cell phone.*

GABE *and* OLIVIA *notice them and sigh.*

CARTER *and* WYATT *appear and escort their wives out for a second time.*

OLIVIA *and* GABE *see that everyone has left, again, and seize the moment! They sprint to the door, bolting all of the locks.*

Finally alone, they smile at each other and kiss again.

Fade to Black.)

End of Play.

OTHER TITLES AVAILABLE FROM SAMUEL FRENCH

NANA'S NAUGHTY KNICKERS

Katherine DiSavino

Comedy / 3m, 5f, 1 m or f / Interior Set

Bridget and her Grandmother are about to become roommates. However, what Bridget saw as a unique opportunity to stay with her favorite Nana in New York for the summer quickly turns into an experience she'll never forget. It seems her sweet Grandma is running an illegal boutique from her apartment, selling hand-made naughty knickers to every senior citizen in the five borough area!

Will Bridget be able to handle all the excitement? Will her Nana get arrested – or worse! – evicted?

"Nana's Naughty Knickers is a slick comedy by a new playwright, Katy DiSavino…the dialog is crisp and funny, and the action fast-paced…[this] Senior Citizen's sexy sideline will have you in stitches!"
– *Lancaster Journal*

"Audiences may laugh themselves right out of their knickers…[the play] flows in a perfect rhythm, and hits every high and low note of comedy."
– *The Dayton Examiner*

SAMUEL FRENCH STAFF

Nate Collins
President

Ken Dingledine
Director of Operations,
Vice President

Bruce Lazarus
Executive Director,
General Counsel

Rita Maté
Director of Finance

ACCOUNTING

Lori Thimsen | Director of Licensing Compliance
Nehal Kumar | Senior Accounting Associate
Charles Graytok | Accounting and Finance Manager
Glenn Halcomb | Royalty Administration
Jessica Zheng | Accounts Receivable
Andy Lian | Accounts Payable
Charlie Sou | Accounting Associate
Joann Mannello | Orders Administrator

BUSINESS AFFAIRS

Caitlin Bartow | Assistant to the Executive Director

CORPORATE COMMUNICATIONS

Abbie Van Nostrand | Director of Corporate
Communications

CUSTOMER SERVICE AND LICENSING

Brad Lohrenz | Director of Licensing Development
Laura Lindson | Licensing Services Manager
Kim Rogers | Theatrical Specialist
Matthew Akers | Theatrical Specialist
Ashley Byrne | Theatrical Specialist
Jennifer Carter | Theatrical Specialist
Annette Storckman | Theatrical Specialist
Julia Izumi | Theatrical Specialist
Sarah Weber | Theatrical Specialist
Nicholas Dawson | Theatrical Specialist
David Kimple | Theatrical Specialist
Ryan McLeod | Theatrical Specialist

EDITORIAL

Amy Rose Marsh | Literary Manager
Ben Coleman | Literary Associate

MARKETING

Ryan Pointer | Marketing Manager
Courtney Kochuba | Marketing Associate
Chris Kam | Marketing Associate

PUBLICATIONS AND PRODUCT DEVELOPMENT

Joe Ferreira | Product Development Manager
David Geer | Publications Manager
Charlyn Brea | Publications Associate
Tyler Mullen | Publications Associate
Derek P. Hassler | Musical Products Coordinator
Zachary Orts | Musical Materials Coordinator

OPERATIONS

Casey McLain | Operations Supervisor
Elizabeth Minski | Office Coordinator, Reception
Coryn Carson | Office Coordinator, Reception

SAMUEL FRENCH BOOKSHOP (LOS ANGELES)

Joyce Mehess | Bookstore Manager
Cory DeLair | Bookstore Buyer
Kristen Springer | Customer Service Manager
Tim Coultas | Bookstore Associate
Bryan Jansyn | Bookstore Associate
Alfred Contreras | Shipping & Receiving

LONDON OFFICE

Anne-Marie Ashman | Accounts Assistant
Felicity Barks | Rights & Contracts Associate
Steve Blacker | Bookshop Associate
David Bray | Customer Services Associate
Robert Cooke | Assistant Buyer
Stephanie Dawson | Amateur Licensing Associate
Simon Ellison | Retail Sales Manager
Robert Hamilton | Amateur Licensing Associate
Peter Langdon | Marketing Manager
Louise Mappley | Amateur Licensing Associate
James Nicolau | Despatch Associate
Emma Anacootee-Parmar | Production/Editorial
Controller
Martin Phillips | Librarian
Panos Panayi | Company Accountant
Zubayed Rahman | Despatch Associate
Steve Sanderson | Royalty Administration Supervisor
Douglas Schatz | Acting Executive Director
Roger Sheppard | I.T. Manager
Debbie Simmons | Licensing Sales Team Leader
Peter Smith | Amateur Licensing Associate
Garry Spratley | Customer Service Manager
David Webster | UK Operations Director
Sarah Wolf | Rights Director